Betty's Not Well Today

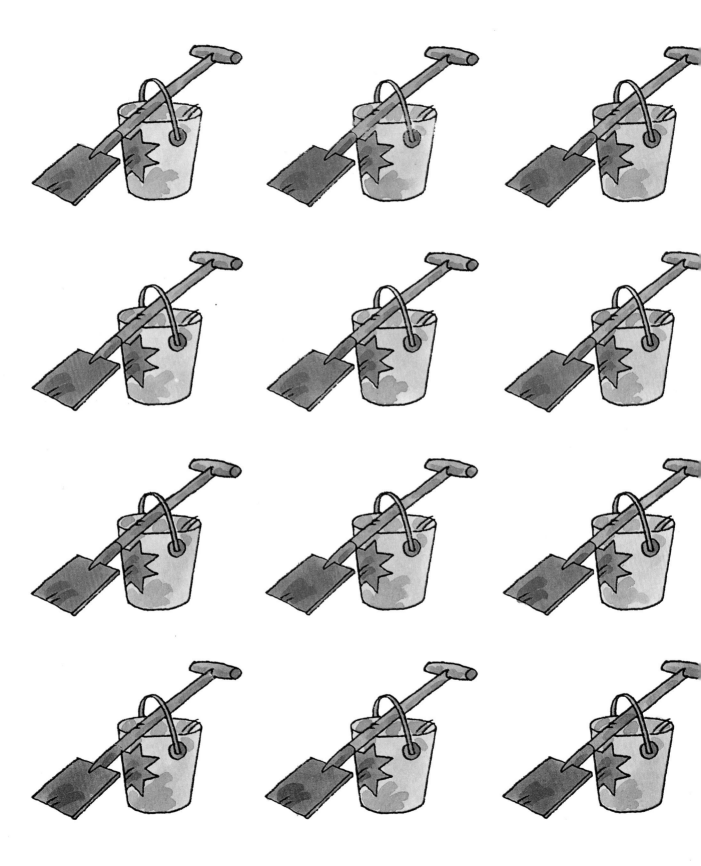

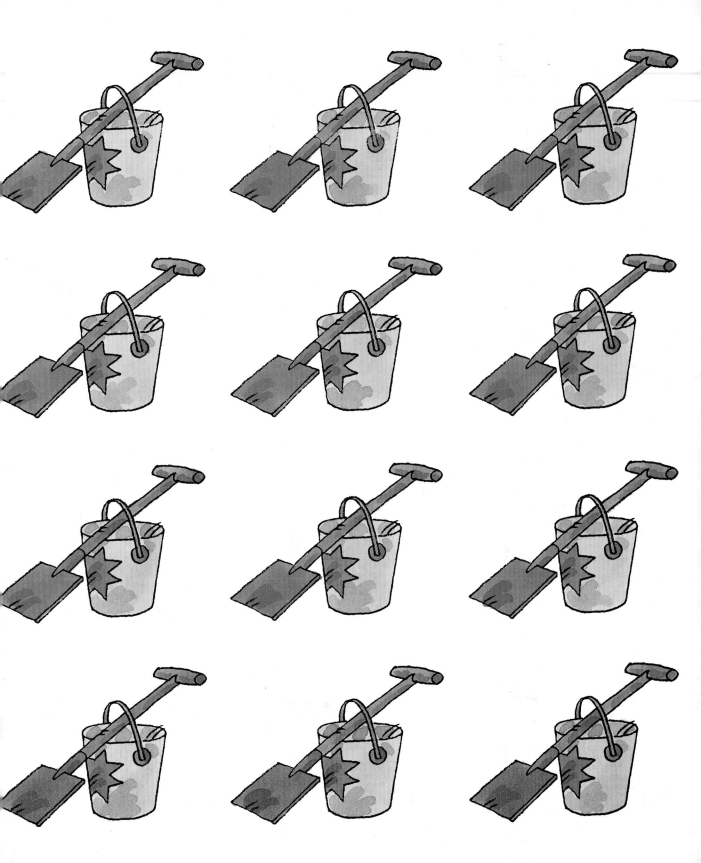

For Owen and Sarah

Betty's Not Well Today

Written and illustrated by
Gus Clarke

Andersen Press · London

She was fine last night when her
friends came to tea. And everyone
else was OK, after jelly and
sausages, ice-cream and beans.

But Betty's not well today.

She might have been sailing way out on the sea,

or climbing the rocks in the bay,

or digging for treasure deep down in the sand.

But Betty's not well today.

She might have been hunting for tigers

and got lost in the jungle with Dad.

She might have gone down for a look at the fair,
and picked up her friends on the way.

She might have won prizes,

or just had a giggle.

But Betty's not well today.

Ah, here comes the doctor. We'll see what *he's* got to say.

Good news!

Betty should soon be up and about,
after a good night's rest. So we'll just wait
and see what the morning will bring.

Let's all hope for the best. . . . Fingers crossed!

Hello. Can't stop. There's a lot to catch up on.
We're just on our way out to play.

But I'm happy to tell you that *I'm* feeling fine,

More Andersen Press paperback picture books!

Scarecrow's Hat
by Ken Brown

The Big Sneeze
by Ruth Brown

Funny Fred
by Peta Coplans

Dear Daddy
by Philippe Dupasquier

War and Peas
by Michael Foreman

Princess Camomile Gets Her Way
by Hiawyn Oram and Susan Varley

Bear's Eggs
by Dieter and Ingrid Schubert

Rabbit's Wish
by Paul Stewart and Chris Riddell

The Sand Horse
by Ann Turnbull and Michael Foreman

Dr Xargle's Book of Earth Hounds
by Jeanne Willis and Tony Ross